the BRAVE CHICKEN

written by
Scott Wyler

illustrated by
Debby Wyler

The Brave Chicken
Copyright © 2020 by Scott Wyler

First Edition

Hardcover ISBN: 978-1-64990-117-0
Paperback ISBN: 978-1-64990-905-3
eBook ISBN: 978-1-64990-192-7

Dedicated with love
to our grandson
Herman

There was a chicken who wanted to be brave.
That's NO way for a chicken to behave.

He thought, "What could I do that would be brave?
I know! I know! I'LL EXPLORE A CAVE!

He was so pleased with the plan he created.
He jumped up and down completely elated.

Never in the history of the world, he believed,
Had a plan like this by a chicken been achieved.

So few brave chickens on the Earth exist.
He might be the only one on the list.

He asked other chickens if they wanted to go.
But every one of them said, "No! No! No!"

Even his best friend, Chicken Dave,
Said, "I will NOT go in a cave."

"If you go in a cave," said Chicken Dave,
"I will stay here and bye-bye I will wave."

The chicken told his plan to his mom and dad.
And they both thought it was REALLY bad.

"You must be kidding," said his dad.
"I thought I raised a smarter lad."

So many tears by his mom were shed.
"How did this plan get into your head?"

"Forget about it and go to bed."
That is what his mother said.

The chicken fell asleep and dreamed of a cave.
He thought, "Exploring a cave is what I crave."

He woke up more determined than ever.
His father said, "Your plan is not clever."

But those words didn't sway the chicken.
He said, "With my plan I will be stickin'."

His mom said, "You have lots of pluck.
But why can't you JUST SIT AND CLUCK?"

He said, "Other chickens can sit and cluck.
The thought of that makes me go, 'YUCK!'"

His dad said, "You're making your life a muck.
Now be a good chicken and SIT AND CLUCK!"

His parents thought his mind wasn't clear.
His mother said, "We love you my dear."

"And we hope you will not be too annoyed,
But we're taking you to see Doctor Chicken Freud."

"He's by far the best in his field.
He'll check you out and get you healed."

The doctor had the chicken lay on a couch.
To the chicken he seemed like a grumpy grouch.

He asked many questions and scribbled on a pad.
It was not the best time the chicken ever had.

In the end the doctor had this to say:
"Here's the decision I've made today."

"It's my opinion that no ifs, ands, or buts,
You're a good chicken but your plan is nuts!"

"I wanted to help you and I tried,
But I think your chicken brain is fried."

However, I'm not one to pass the buck.
My advice to you is JUST SIT AND CLUCK!"

The chicken left and his parents were happy.
"That puts an end to this," said his pappy.

The brave chicken had no "quit."
So he was swayed not one bit.

He told that to his girlfriend, Chicken Charlene.
The prettiest chicken you've ever seen.

But his cave plan seemed to ruffle her feathers.
She said, "This could affect our get-togethers."

She told him, "If you do your stupid cave plan,
I will find myself another chicken man."

He said, "Chicken Charlene, do what you must.
But my cave plan I will not adjust."

She said, "With a wacko chicken I'm stuck.
Why won't you JUST SIT AND CLUCK?"

Chicken Charlene left very mad.
And the chicken now felt so sad.

When next he saw her she was with Chicken Dave.
And she said, "Chicken Dave is now my fave."

It hurt the chicken to hear her rave,
About his ex-best friend, Chicken Dave.

When he realized he had been jilted,
His eyes got wet and his flower wilted.

Word of his plan spread from chicken to chicken.
And his reputation was takin' a lickin'.

All of the chickens were laughing at him.
They said, "There's that chicken who's so dim."

They called him stupid and foolish and crazy.
They said the inside of his brain was hazy.

No one seemed to be a fan,
Of his cave exploring plan.

Chicken Dave told him, "There's no doubt,
You for sure will chicken out."

"Just watch me go!" the chicken said.
"I'm off to the cave full speed ahead."

Then the chicken boldly strode,
Right across a two-lane road.

"Chicken, why did you cross the road?" Dave cried.
"To get to the other side," he replied.

Chicken Dave said, "You're such a stupe!
I can't believe you flew the coop."

"You could've been hit by a truck.
Now come back here and SIT AND CLUCK!"

The chicken was thinking, "Wow!
I'm a free range chicken now!"

Then he walked a long, long way,
Which took up a big part of the day.

Down deep valleys and up steep hills.
Suffering many falls and spills.

But suddenly he thought, "Oh no, oh dear!
I have a bit of a problem I fear."

"One small detail could affect this biz.
I HAVE NO IDEA WHERE A CAVE IS!"

"It possibly would have been smart,
To have thought of that at the start."

The chicken was in deep despair.
"Where is a cave? Oh where, oh where?"

A butterfly flew down to him.
She said, "You're looking kind of grim."

"I'm searching for a cave," he declared.
"I should've been much more prepared."

The butterfly said, "I fly to many spots.
So I see lots and lots and lots."

"And I happen to definitely for sure know,
That if you want a cave over there you go."

"Thank you," said the chicken as she flew away.
Then he ran in that direction without delay.

And soon before his eyes he saw,
A cave that filled him full of awe.

The once brave chicken was now a nervous wreck.
He said, "I might have bit off more than I can peck."

Seeing the big cave made his heartbeat quicken.
He thought, "Oh no, I'M A CHICKEN CHICKEN!"

He wondered, "Should I go in or should I not?
It depends on how much courage I've got."

Slowly he entered the very large space.
Never before had he seen such a place.

Just one step in he felt such fright.
The cave was cold and dark as night.

His eyes soon adjusted and then he saw,
Something that made him want to withdraw.

It had big wings and a tiny head.
The bravest chicken would've felt dread.

For some odd reason it was hanging upside down.
And next to it was a bird colored orange and brown.

"Who are you?" asked the scared chicken,
Whose face now looked very stricken.

The creature said, "I'm a bat, man, and this is Robin."
"We're just hanging out here hobnobbin'."

The bat seemed like a pretty good guy.
The chicken said, "I'm just passing by."

The bat said, "Enjoy your time in here.
Make sure you say hello to the bear."

"A bear?" the shaking chicken replied.
Then he headed further inside.

And yes there was a bear.
Sitting on a rock chair.

"Hi," said the chicken to the big bear.
The chicken again was feeling fear.

"Hi," said the bear who sat on a rock.
"Do you know the time? I have no clock."

The chicken said, "Yes, in fact I do.
The time right now is nine thirty two."

"Thanks," said the bear, "I hibernate here.
I live in here five months a year."

The chicken and the bear in the chair had a chat,
Then the chicken said bye to the bear, bird and bat.

Though now he was quite enjoying this place,
It was time for him to get back to his base.

The cheerful chicken ran all the way back.
He did not even stop for a snack.

He had just achieved his goal.
And it pleased his chicken soul.

"I DID IT! I DID IT!" he gave a loud yell.
"I followed my dream and it went swell!"

He reached Chicken Town and the chickens were there.
The chickens had gathered in Chicken Town Square.

When the chickens saw the chicken they all cheered.
And the chicken thought, "That was really weird."

Chicken Charlene was there.
She was leading the cheer.

"Why are you cheering for me?" the chicken asked.
While in their attention he happily basked.

"YOU EXPLORED A CAVE!" yelled Chicken Charlene.
"You're the bravest chicken we've ever seen!"

She said, "You went in and didn't run away!"
Then the other chickens yelled, "HIP-HIP HOORAY!"

The brave chicken asked, "How did you know?
Chicken Charlene said, "She told us so."

She pointed to a butterfly dancing in the sky."
Then she said, "You're an amazing guy!"

Some chickens lifted the chicken in the air.
And even Chicken Dave was there.

Doctor Chicken Freud was also in the pack.
He said, "My previous opinion I take back."

Then said his smiling mom and dad:
"You're a chicken who makes us glad."

"Speech, speech, speech!" the chickens chanted.
And their request would be granted.

The brave chicken said, "You're all out of luck,
If you think I'll ever just sit and cluck!

Be like the brave chicken and follow your dream.
It's not as impossible as it may seem.

Others might say that you won't succeed.
But your opinion is all you need.

THE END

TAKE THE BRAVE CHICKEN VOW.
<u>SAY IT LOUD THEN TAKE A BOW.</u>

Cheep, cheep, cheep, cheep, cheep, cheep, cheep!
This is a promise that I will keep.

Like the brave chicken, here's what I say,
I will follow my dream every day.

And as just a bit of a refresher,
I won't be swayed by peer pressure.

Cheep, cheep, cheep, cheep, cheep, cheep, cheep!
I'm a brave chicken and not a sheep.

CPSIA information can be obtained
at www.ICGtesting.com
Printed in the USA
LVHW071130140121
676450LV00022B/705